MAKING THE GRADE
An Adolescent's Struggle
with Attention Deficit Disorder

by

Roberta N. Parker

Featuring

Commonly Asked Questions
About Attention Deficit Disorder

by

Harvey C. Parker, Ph.D.

Illustrations by
Richard A. DiMatteo

Specialty Press, Inc.
Plantation, Florida

To my family

Library of Congress Catalog Card Number 92-070274
Parker, Roberta N. and Parker, Harvey C.
Making the Grade: An Adolescent's Struggle With
Attention Deficit Disorder / by Roberta N. Parker and
Harvey C. Parker
p. 48   cm.

Summary: A heartwarming story of a young teenager's
efforts to overcome problems associated with attention deficit
disorder.

ISBN 0-9621629-1-4 (paper)

1. Attention deficit disorder- Treatment-Juvenile literature
2. Hyperactivity- Treatment -Juvenile literature

Published by Specialty Press, Inc. 300 NW 70th Avenue
Plantation, Florida 33317 (305) 792-8944.

Manufactured in the United States of America

10 9 8 7 6 5 4 3 2 1

CONTENTS

RESOURCES.. 4

CHAPTER ONE... 5

CHAPTER TWO.. 9

CHAPTER THREE.................................... 13

CHAPTER FOUR...................................... 17

CHAPTER FIVE.. 21

CHAPTER SIX.. 25

CHAPTER SEVEN.................................... 29

COMMONLY ASKED QUESTIONS
ABOUT ADD... 33

Resources

**Other Books and Videos About Attention Deficit Disorders
For Young Children and Teens**

Gehret, Jeanne. (1991) *Eagle Eyes.* New York. Verbal Images
    Press.
Goldstein, S. and Goldstein, M. (1991) *It's Just Attention
    Disorder: A Video For Kids.* Utah. Neurology, Learn-
    ing and Behavior Center.
Gordon, M. (1991). *Jumpin' Johnny Get Back To Work.* New
    York. Gordon Publications, Inc.
Gordon, M. (1991). *My Brother's A World Class Pain.* New
    York. Gordon Publications, Inc.
Levine, M. (1990). *Getting A Head In School. A Student's
    Book About Learning Abilities and Learning Disorders.*
    Cambridge, MA. Educator's Publishing Service.
Nadeau, K. and Dixon, E. (1991) *Learning To Slow Down and
    Pay Attention.* Virginia. Chesapeake Psychological
    Services.
Parker, R. and Parker, H. (1993) *Slam Dunk: A Young Boy's
    Struggle with Attention Deficit Disorder.* Florida.
    Specialty Press, Inc.
Quinn, P. O. and Stern, J.M. (1991). *Putting On The Brakes.
    Young People's Guide To Understanding Attention
    Deficit Hyperactivity Disorder (ADHD).* New York.
    Magination Press.

All of the above products are available through the
A.D.D.WareHouse. For more information about these and
other products related to ADD, or to receive a free catalog call
or write:
A.D.D. WareHouse
300 Northwest 70th Avenue
Plantation, Florida 33317
(800) ADD-WARE • (305) 792-8944

CHAPTER
ONE

The alarm clock just sounded at the Jerome household. It was 7:00 AM on a beautiful September morning.

Mrs. Jerome called out to her daughter, Kate, who was asleep in her bedroom down the hall, "Kate, time to get up for school."

Kate awoke eager to begin her first day as a 9th grader at Central Junior High School. Her clothes were all ready as she had carefully selected them the night before so this morning could be carefree and she could fully enjoy the excitement that the first day of a school year brings.

Kate's mom put on her robe and slippers and ventured out of her bedroom to the room next to Kate's. She quietly opened the door and said in a soft voice, "Jim it's time to get up and get ready for junior high school." This was to be Jim's first day at Central Junior High School. He was starting 7th grade.

"Mom!" exclaimed Jim, "Is it 7:00 o'clock already?"

Mom smiled sweetly and replied, "Jim, this will be a very challenging and interesting day for you. Now, get dressed and come directly to the kitchen for breakfast.

You need to be ready on time to walk to the bus with Kate."

Jim knew exactly what to wear. He rehearsed the routine of getting ready for school last night. He laid out his clothes, including his new athletic shoes and socks. He even filled a bookbag with notebooks, pens and pencils and he put his lunch money right in the pocket of his trousers. Mom wanted so badly for the day to go smoothly for Jim and for him to like junior high school. Jim, in turn, wanted so badly to please mom. For the past few days he and mom and dad had some pretty serious talks about him becoming more responsible and all agreed that this was the year that would set the tone for how successful he would be in school.

His clothes went on and it was smooth sailing so far. Now, a short trip to the bathroom to wash up and he would be in the kitchen eating breakfast in no time at all.

Unfortunately, when he entered the bathroom, he was in such a hurry that he accidentally knocked over the mouthwash and found himself standing in an aqua puddle which was soaking his athletic shoes. "What next?" yelped Jim. But, he pulled it together, calmed himself, used some toweling to clean up his shoes, and he was back in business. Now, what business was that? He seemed to have momentarily forgotten his goal to get ready for breakfast and started to refill the mouthwash bottle with some soapy water. He thought this was a cute little joke, if Kate fell for it and used the "mouthwash."

Luckily, Kate was saved as mom called to him, "Jim, hurry up, you don't want to be late your first day." He dispensed with the idea of creative mouthwash and finished up in the bathroom. In a flash, Jim was in the kitchen eating breakfast. Mrs. Jerome was as happy as a lark as dad looked on.

Mr. Jerome wasn't much of a morning person. The tensions of his job seemed to keep him preoccupied in the mornings. In past school years, Jim's morning diversions always served to upset him. They reminded him of all the thoughtless pranks his own brother Frank put him through when he was a boy. Fortunately, he was un-aware of this morning's mouthwash incident and was reflecting Mrs. Jerome's good mood.

It was time. Kate and Jim gathered their belong-ings and made way for the door. Mom turned to them and said, "Have a great day Kate. Jim, good luck, and do as you are told, and don't get lost on your way to the bus, and keep your mind on your work and ..."

Then dad had his turn wishing Kate well and preaching another sermon to Jim, just as his mother did. For the finale, they both wished Kate and Jim a good day one more time.

Jim couldn't help but think about the farewells. He knew their concerns were well-founded.

CHAPTER
TWO

As they started toward the bus stop Kate said, "Come on, Jim, don't be upset. They didn't mean anything by that. Mom and dad are just so nervous because it's your first day." Then Kate gave him a little smile of approval. Jim thought to himself, she will never know how much those little smiles mean to me.

His spirit rose once again and a feeling of excitement and eagerness came over him. "This is my first day of junior high school and it's going to be great!" Jim shouted. Kate smiled again.

They were closer to the bus stop now, and Kate recognized some of her friends waiting for her. She soon forgot that she was with Jim and joined them. Jim understood, but it left him with nothing to occupy his mind. He looked and looked, but didn't see anyone he knew. So, he drifted a little way down the street to give himself a better view of some of the side streets. That way, he would know if anyone familiar was coming. He was so involved looking down the street that he had to rush back to the stop to make the bus.

As students boarded the bus, Kate suddenly remembered her almost forgotten brother and helped him on. Jim was a little nervous when he got on the bus. Kate showed no signs of emotion as these diversions of Jim's were fairly routine. She was a bit surprised at Jim's nervousness, but she just chalked it up to being the first day and gave him another smile.

The bus made several stops along the way. Kate greeted more kids. She seemed to know everyone. Jim sat in his seat and played with the strap on his bookbag as he studied all the new faces. He felt proud of his sister's popularity and wondered if he would be able to make a lot of friends in his new school.

While fiddling with the strap on his bookbag, his hand wandered a little to the side and accidentally poked the boy in the seat next to him. What a great time for an introduction! Jim said, "Hi!, my name is Jim Jerome. What's yours?"

"Billy Hoover" answered the prospective friend. "Is this your first year of junior high?" asked Billy.

Nervously Jim said, "Yes, sure thing." Jim couldn't seem to find the right words to explain just how excited he was feeling. As it happened, they had lots in common given that Billy was also a newcomer to the school.

The bus finally arrived at school and it was time to disembark. Kate leaned toward Jim and said, "Have fun" as she gave him one more smile for the road. Jim was hoping for more than just a smile this time. Kate, however, was soon out of sight.

Jim had the aisle seat and Billy waited patiently for him to get up so they could leave the bus. Everyone was out of their seats and off the bus. Finally, Billy said, "Jim, we have to go now." Jim was so nervous he just kept talking. Both had a good laugh and scurried toward the school yard. When they determined that they were in the same class, Jim was more relaxed because he knew he had met someone he liked. Billy turned out to be a decent guy in Jim's eyes. He felt they could be good friends. Together they found their way to class.

CHAPTER
THREE

Billy looked back at Jim and waited to see his face as Mrs. Singer, their homeroom teacher, made the morning announcements. This morning ritual was usually fairly boring, but today it was special.

Eight weeks of junior high school had passed. Mrs. Singer spoke, "Today students, your last class will be dismissed ten minutes early at which time you will return to homeroom to pick up your report cards. They are to be signed by your parents tonight and returned to me tomorrow morning."

Jim momentarily felt his heart sink. Billy was still looking at him and smiling. Jim wondered if Billy was as worried as he was.

The bell rang and without a word, both boys walked to their first class. Jim took his seat. Again, Billy was nearby. Their names, Hoover and Jerome, kept them alphabetically close to each other in all of their classes. Jim always felt that to be a blessing, but today he thought it might be nice to have a little privacy.

As the day wore on, Jim became more and more anxious. Report cards had almost always been a problem in elementary school and he wondered if things would change now. As usual, this feeling of uneasiness made him nervous and he acted very fidgety. Several of his teachers reminded him throughout the day to sit still.

During his last period of class Jim began to ponder over Coach Richard's words, "You are a fast swimmer with very good form. Since you are only a seventh grader, you can be a wonderful asset to the school swim team for the next three years." When the Coach told him that at the first swim practice, Jim felt like he was standing on top of the world. Wow! What a feeling. But then, Coach went on to say; "Your swimming will keep up and improve with diligent practice. I know you can do that. So

Jim, make sure you keep up your grades and stay out of trouble. School policy dictates that you must be a student in very good standing to be on a school team. Remember, you'll have to make the grade."

At the time, Jim thought Coach's directives wouldn't be too hard to follow. Jim wondered whether today would be the day of reckoning. Being on the team was so wonderful. Even the older teammates respected him. For that matter, lots of the kids knew his name and would say hello to him. Dad was so proud. Mom and Kate just beamed whenever they talked about how well he had adjusted to school. Jim asked himself, "Will I still be a student in good standing after today? Will I make the grade?"

On the way back to homeroom, Billy asked Jim, "Jim, what's going on? You are acting like some strange dude today. I almost don't know it's you."

Jim responded, "I guess I'm a little nervous about report cards. Aren't you?" Billy knew that he was doing well. He was a very good student who enjoyed drama club as much as Jim loved swimming. Everything at school was going well for Billy and he knew it.

Anyway, Billy replied, "No, and don't you worry about it either. We'll both do fine. Just try to pay attention more. You're having an off-day, that's all."

But Jim thought back and remembered that he had had lots of off days. He remained worried even with Billy's encouragement.

Once everyone was seated in homeroom, Mrs. Singer asked for quiet. She had a stack of envelopes in her hand. The report cards were inside. When everyone finally quieted down, she distributed them. Jim looked around and watched the kids expressions as they opened the envelopes. Mrs. Singer said, "Please don't discuss your grades with your classmates. It is best to put the cards back in the envelopes and give them to your parents. Class dismissed!"

Billy sensed Jim's uneasiness and didn't ask him about his grades. Together they boarded their bus.

CHAPTER
FOUR

A few days had passed and Jim found himself and his parents sitting in Mrs. Jones' office. Mrs. Jones was the school guidance counselor. She was a tall, attractive woman with a gentle smile and a very neat office.

In her office was a large conference table around which they sat. Mrs. Jones said, "I am so pleased that you could meet with us today." Jim knew she was really speaking to his parents, but somehow she made him feel included. "The teachers will be here momentarily" she confirmed.

In walked Jim's math teacher, followed by his English, social studies, science and physical education teachers. His physical education teacher also happened to be his swim coach and now Jim was becoming noticeably uncomfortable. His fidgeting began.

While Mrs. Jones politely introduced all of Jim's teachers to his parents, Jim became more distracted and began to loudly tap his foot on the base of the conference table. Mom said, "Jim, control yourself." Suddenly, Jim became aware of what he was doing and quieted himself.

All of Jim's teachers smiled and greeted him. They all knew him and realized that he had the same problem in class. It didn't take much for Jim to become distracted and lose his focus on the lesson. While he was focusing on something other than the lesson, he often made enough noise to disrupt the class. So, not only was he not learning, but he was hindering his classmates from learning as well.

Each of his teachers took the opportunity to speak to him and his parents, but they all really said the same thing. They explained that Jim was well liked and bright, but somehow he could not finish the work he started because he would become distracted and do something other than the task at hand.

BEHAVIOR RATING SCALE

Name **Jim Jerome**   Grade **7**

Rate the student on each of the following:

	Not At all	Just a Little	Pretty Much	Very Much
1. Has trouble paying attention				✓
2. Cannot concentrate on assigned work			✓	
3. Impulsive; impatient			✓	
4. Difficulty keeping work organized			✓	
5. Has trouble sitting still; fidgets				✓
6. Difficulty finishing work			✓	
7. Tries hard to solve difficult work			✓	
8. Starts fights with others	✓			
9. Short attention span				✓
10. Gets upset easily		✓		

Mrs. Jones provided some forms that were filled out by all of Jim's teachers and his parents. She said, "Based on our meeting here today and Jim's behavior as reported in these forms, I believe Jim has an attention problem. I would like Jim to meet with a psychologist for further evaluation."

At that point, Jim's dad sighed and his mom looked worried. Mrs. Jones was kind and reassuring. She told them the evaluation was a simple process and if Jim had an attention problem, they could all work together to help him.

Coach Richards asked if the school could make an exception and allow Jim to remain on the swim team until they could resolve this problem. Mrs. Jones said, "Yes." without any hesitation.

Jim and his parents left the conference feeling

very hopeful. Jim wanted nothing more than to do well in school. Together, they would get the help Jim needed to make the grade. Jim felt very encouraged.

CHAPTER
FIVE

When the Jerome's returned home, Mrs. Jerome called their family doctor, Dr. Flint, and told him about the school conference. Dr. Flint had known Jim since he was a baby. He agreed that it would be a good idea for Jim to see a psychologist and told Jim's mother that they were not alone with this problem. He had treated several other youngsters who had attention problems. This information made Jim's mother feel much more comfortable. He then told her to call Dr. Bross, a local psychologist who works with children and adolescents.

Kate remembered hearing of Dr. Bross. One of her friends visited Dr. Bross when she had some problems back in 7th grade. Kate told Jim about her friend and said, "Jim, I think you are pretty lucky to have all of these people so interested in helping you. You must be doing something right." Then, she smiled at him and added, "My friend is doing great now." Jim felt right for the first time all day.

The visit to Dr. Bross's office was actually very pleasant. Dr. Bross was a warm friendly man. His warmth made Jim and his parents glad that they came to see him. Jim's parents shared lots of stories with Dr. Bross about Jim's behavior. He explained that he would administer several psychological tests and afterwards he would discuss the results with them.

The testing lasted for a few hours. It was different from any tests Jim had taken in school. Dr. Bross would ask questions and he would answer. It was like having a conversation. Jim felt good about being with Dr. Bross. He worked out puzzles, had a chance to work on a computer and even had his memory tested. Although Jim was a little tired when the testing was finished, he had had an enjoyable morning.

The Jerome's returned the next afternoon to learn the results of the testing. Since Jim's last meeting with Dr. Bross, Dr. Bross had called the school and had spoken with Jim's teachers. At this meeting, Dr. Bross explained that as a result of the testing and speaking with Jim's parents and teachers, he determined that Jim had an Attention Deficit Disorder commonly known as ADD. He said that 3-5% of the population suffered with this disorder. Youngsters like Jim who were diagnosed as having this problem could be helped by their parents and teachers to do better in school. He suggested to Jim's parents that they help structure his homework by helping him break it down into parts with Jim taking a break between parts.

Dr. Bross said, "Jim is very bright and very capable of completing his assignments correctly. The problem is that kids with ADD are easily distracted and have trouble paying attention for long periods of time." He continued, "That's why in the past Jim would have trouble finishing his classwork and homework. Naturally, this would cause him to fall very far behind and he wouldn't have time to finish his work."

When speaking with Jim's teachers, Dr. Bross suggested that they help Jim by giving him shorter assignments and having him sit closer to the front of the classroom. He recommended that they write the assignments on the board for Jim so if he forgot what they said he could copy the assignments and catch up. All of Jim's teachers were eager to cooperate because Jim was well liked by them. Now they understood why Jim was so fidgety and easily distracted and they all wanted to help.

Child's Name_____

Teacher: _____

Week of _____

Goal Card	MON.	TUES.	WED.	THURS.	FRI.
1. Paid attention in class					
2. Completed work in class					
3. Completed homework					
4. Was well behaved					
5. Desk & notebook neat					
Totals					
Teacher's Initials					

N/A — Not applicable   1 — Poor   4 — Good
O — Losing, forgetting or destroy-   2 — Needs Improvement   5 — Excellent
    ing card   3 — Fair

Dr. Bross then explained that the psychologist's role was to help Jim alter his behavior by being more aware of what he does. Jim and Dr. Bross made up a behavior chart. Dr. Bross told Jim to have each of his teachers check whether or not he was completing his work each day.

Before the meeting ended, Dr. Bross explained there was yet another way to manage ADD. "Medications are oftentimes used with children and teenagers who have ADD to help them pay attention" said Dr. Bross. He told the Jim's parents that they should call Dr. Flint and ask him if he felt Jim could benefit from taking medicine like Ritalin to help him do better in school. He explained that kids who took ADD medication found it easier to pay attention and complete assignments.

Mr. and Mrs. Jerome welcomed Dr. Bross's advice and agreed to call Dr. Flint, who later prescribed Ritalin for Jim.

CHAPTER
SIX

Jim was just finishing the last problem on a math test, when his teacher announced, "Class, you have three more minutes to review your papers, then it's pencils down." A feeling of relief came over him. He felt so confident as he looked back at the questions and checked his answers. There was even time for a quick glance at Billy. He too seemed to be reviewing his paper.

Last grading period Jim never finished a math test. He just couldn't concentrate. Now he was able to stick with it. The charts Dr. Bross gave him really helped. It seemed that all of his teachers tried to make the assignments easier for him to complete. Jim was feeling as though his teachers liked him. They were all so encouraging when he finished his work. Even the kids were nicer to him. Perhaps, he wasn't so annoying anymore since he was fidgeting less and being less disruptive.

Class was over and all of the test papers were collected. Billy asked, "Jim, what did you think?"

"Not so bad," replied Jim. "How about you?"

"I think I did O.K.," said Billy. Modest comments

like that meant both thought they got all the answers right.

Together, they walked to the cafeteria for lunch. The lunch line didn't look too long, so they rushed to it before the crowds came. The smell of the chili was strong and lots of kids were joking about the effect it might have on their health. Jim always enjoyed joking about the school food, but he ate it anyway. So did Billy.

After making their way through the lunch line, they took their trays to a nearby table. Some of the guys and girls from the swim team were sitting at this table. Jim got a big hello from them and he felt great. He knew, he was becoming popular, just like Kate.

It felt good to have friends and Jim felt especially lucky to have met Billy. Since Jim was seeing Dr. Bross and following his advice, he noticed that the kids liked him more and he was making new friends. He also noticed that when he took his Ritalin dose he felt calmer and it was easier to make conversation. Billy was his friend since day one. He had always been tolerant of Jim's diversions, but now Jim felt even closer to Billy. Jim recognized that Billy had always been a good listener, a quality that he now appreciated and was able to demonstrate as well.

As they ate their lunch, Billy told Jim that he was up for a part in the school play. Jim listened intently. He said "Wow, Billy I really hope you make it. I know it will be a better play with you in it." Billy punched him playfully in the arm. That was Billy's way of thanking Jim for being a terrific friend and Jim knew it.

Lunch had to be the fastest period of the day. "Time just flies when you are having fun." announced the lunchroom teacher. "So, clear your trays and return to class". None of the kids enjoyed the humor, but they followed the directive nonetheless.

As he and Billy made their way down the hallway, he felt someone tugging at his arm. It was Lauren. She was a booster for the swim team. Jim often saw her at practice, since she was there rehearsing.

Lauren was a slender girl with long dark hair and big brown eyes. Jim thought she was very pretty, but he never told this to anyone, not even Billy. Of course, he just recently started to notice her, as prior to his seeing Dr. Bross, he never looked at her long enough to notice that she was both cute and friendly. He would be too busy with other diversions.

Anyway, Lauren asked Jim, "This weekend I am having a party to celebrate my birthday. Will you and Billy be able to come?"

Jim said, "Sure."

Billy said, "I'd like to, but I need to ask my folks. Can I tell you tomorrow?"

Lauren replied, "Fine, I hope you both can come."

"Thanks." shouted the guys.

Then Jim remembered, "Gee, Billy I guess I have to ask my parents too, but I think they'll say yes. They better, I already did."

Billy said, "Well maybe you should have thought about it before you answered."

Jim remembered that Dr. Bross told him not to be impulsive. He had problems with that, especially when he was around Lauren. Billy seemed to understand and told him not to worry as his folks would say yes and so would Billy's.

CHAPTER
SEVEN

Jim entered his house only to find out that his mom wasn't home. All afternoon he thought of how he would go about asking her for permission to attend the party. While he anticipated that his mother, who was always kind and understanding, would say yes, he couldn't be sure. Having to wait for her to come home only served to bring on anxiety.

As he passed through the house, he heard some noises coming from the study. He looked in and saw dad sitting behind his desk doing some paperwork. Mr. Jerome looked up and said "Hello, son, come on in."

Jim went in and sat down. He was a little surprised. Usually, when his father was working, he didn't want Jim around. Jim's fidgeting always irritated him. But, today dad seemed so happy to see him.

"Jim, I have been wanting to talk to you" said dad. "Looking back at the time that has passed since your last report card, so much has happened" he continued. "Your mother and I are so pleased with the way you get yourself ready for school and take responsibility for completing your work."

Jim thought about what he was saying and realized that by following Dr. Bross's advice, he really was doing better. Jim recognized that he was more focused, able to set goals, and rate his performances. The psychologist called it self-monitoring. Whatever the name, knowing that he was rating himself really helped him follow through. He knew that he couldn't ever answer to a higher authority than his own conscience.

Dad went on "We are so proud of your accomplishments on the swim team. You have worked so hard and your teammates and coach really respect you. At the last meet, you thrilled us all with your win in the distance competition. We knew you were fast, but now we know you have stamina too."

"Thanks, dad!" Jim exclaimed and thought this is the perfect moment to ask if he could have permission to go to the party.

But, just as he tried to speak, dad went on, "Jim, report cards are going to be issued next week." Jim's heart sank. He knew he was doing better, but report cards didn't ever bring happy thoughts, so he might as well forget about going to the party.

Dad came close to him and went on. "I have spoken to Mrs. Jones, your guidance counselor, and she says that after speaking to your teachers..."

Jim interrupted, "But, dad, I tried so hard." He felt so bad. His father sensed his feelings and asked, "Why are you so upset?" "You're doing great." Finally, you are making the grade."

Jim's spirit rose and a feeling of excitement came over him.

In walked mom and Kate. They said, "Hello."

Jim shouted "I'm making the grade!"

Mom said, "That's terrific Jim. If you keep on trying, you can succeed this way for the rest of your life."

Mom and dad were so proud of Jim. So was Kate. Kate smiled at him and he felt great.

This was a perfect time to ask for permission to go to the party and that's just what Jim did.

Commonly Asked Questions About Attention Deficit Disorder
by
Harvey C. Parker, Ph.D.

1. What is attention deficit disorder (ADD)?

ADD is a biological disorder which affects a person's ability to pay attention. Those with ADD usu-

ally have trouble concentrating and at times trouble controlling their behavior. Some individuals with ADD can not sit still for long periods of time without getting restless and fidgety and, in turn, are frequently perceived as hyperactive. Others with ADD are exactly the opposite. While they also have trouble paying attention, they are not considered hyperactive. In fact, they seem to be less active than most and usually take longer to get things done.

ADD can effect a person's life in many ways. It can hinder performance in school, make it difficult to make as well as keep friends, and cause problems at home. Having ADD is no one's fault! With help from parents and teachers and a lot of effort, a person can overcome some of the problems that ADD might cause. Remember, no one is responsible for causing ADD, but if a person has ADD they are responsible for trying to control it.

2. What causes a person to have ADD?

Although no one is sure what exactly causes an attention deficit disorder, some scientists believe it has something to do with the way the body works to control behavior and attention. The brain is a complex information network made up of billions of nerve cells called neurons. Neurons send information to each other in much the same way as signals are transmitted electronically in a telecommunica-

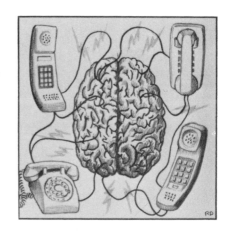

tions network. However, messages within the brain are transferred by substances called neurotransmitter chemicals. People with ADD may not have enough of these chemicals and, therefore, their body has trouble controlling attention and activity.

3. Is ADD inherited?

In some cases, probably yes. Like the color of one's eyes or hair, ADD has been thought to be hereditary. Therefore, most people with ADD were probably born with it. If a person has ADD, there is a high probability that a biological relative has suffered as well from the same condition. Since ADD tends to be more common in boys than in girls, ask some of your male relatives if they ever had trouble paying attention.

4. How else can a person get ADD?

We are not sure of all the ways a person can get ADD. We do know that it isn't contagious, so you can't catch it from someone else. We also know that those who have ADD were probably born with it, unless they had an accident or illness, which could have affected the way their body is able to pay attention and manage their impulses and activity.

5. Does diet make a difference?

That is a rather difficult question to answer and one which many people have argued about for several years. Some scientists believe there is a relationship between what people eat and how they act. They blame certain types of food such as sugar, artificial colorings and preservatives for causing hyperactivity. However, other scientists studied children on many different kinds of diets to see what affect, if any, food would have on behavior. The results seemed to indicate that food has little affect on behavior and for most people it does not cause ADD.   Needless to say, however, if a person has ADD it is a good rule of thumb for them to avoid eating foods which   seem to affect their attention span or behavior.

6. Why does a person have to take medication if they have ADD?

They don't! Taking medication for any illness or condition is a personal decision that obviously requires a great deal of thought along with input from both a physician and one's parents. Keep in mind that for most children and teenagers with ADD, taking medication has been found to help them pay attention, control behavior, and perform more effectively in school. On the other hand, there are those who feel that medication should only be taken when you are sick. Since ADD doesn't make a person feel sick, they do not see the point in taking medication.

Nevertheless, the various medications used to manage ADD have proven to be of enormous benefit because they somehow affect chemicals in the body that help one to pay attention and stay in control. Still, even though it helps to correct a problem, putting something in one's body to effect the way the body reacts is not something a person should do without giving it a great deal of thought.

7. How can medication help?

There are several different kinds of medication that can help children, teens and even adults who have ADD. The most commonly prescribed is Ritalin. When a person with ADD takes Ritalin they often do better in school and on tasks which require them to pay attention. Ritalin reduces hyperactivity and helps control behavior so the person will more likely think things through be-

fore reacting. Since Ritalin improves attention span and helps hyperactive children settle down, teachers often find that ADD students who take Ritalin get more of their work done in school and listen better.

8. What are the side-effects of Ritalin?

Side-effects are the unwanted effects that medication produces in your body. They can sometimes be quite uncomfortable and that is one of the reasons we try to avoid taking medicine unless it is necessary.

For Ritalin, the side-effects vary with the individual. Many children have no side effects whatsoever when they take Ritalin. They don't feel a difference in their bodies at all. Some children, however, may feel uncomfortable when taking Ritalin. It can cause them to have headaches, stomach aches, or lose their appetite for part of the day. Oftentimes these problems go away after a few weeks when their body gets used to the medicine. For some, however, the headaches or stomachaches continue, thus making it necessary to stop the medication. Ritalin has been known to bring about side-effects which are more severe such as irritability, sadness or nervousness. This doesn't happen often, but if it does, tell a doctor. Sometimes lowering the amount of medicine taken or switching to a different medicine will eliminate any negative side-effects.

9. Can medicine cure ADD?

Unfortunately, it can not. The medicines available, however, are pretty good at working for short amounts of time. Ritalin, for example, is effective from four to eight hours depending on the type of Ritalin taken and how it works in a person's body. Since the medicine is usually needed the most during school, and the school day lasts anywhere from six to eight hours, Ritalin is generally taken twice a day. For the best results, your doctor might prescribe that it be taken before school and around noontime.

10. What other medicines can help kids with ADD?

Dexedrine and Cylert are two other medicines which, like Ritalin, are helpful for children, teens and adults with ADD. Dexedrine and Cylert both are members of a group of medications called stimulants. They both are also good at improving attention span and reducing hyperactivity, but they work differently. Dexedrine, like Ritalin, takes effect very quickly, often within thirty minutes after you take it. Cylert, on the other hand, can take three to six weeks to take effect, but it can be effective all day.

Tofranil and Desipramine are two other medications used to help people with ADD. They are members of a class of medicines called anti-depressants and they have been used for many years to treat people who suffer from depression. Fortunately these medicines also can improve ADD.

11. How long do kids with ADD have to take medication?

As a general rule, medication should only be taken for as long as it is necessary. This, of course will vary with each person. One of the interesting things about ADD is it sometimes improves by itself as the person gets older. For instance, young ADD children often have more trouble sitting still and paying attention than do teenagers. Therefore, teenagers can sometimes take less medicine than a younger child might need. Most children who take medicine to manage their attention deficit disorder will use the medicine for several years and maybe longer if they find it helpful. It has recently been discovered that adults who have ADD can be helped by the same medicines that children take.

12. Are there any benefits to having ADD?

Although having ADD can cause many problems, there may be some advantages as well. Many children with ADD have excellent memories for past events that others tend to forget. Hyperactive people are energetic and if they put their energy to good use they can accomplish a lot in a short period of time. Many adults with hyperactivity are quite successful. They never seem to "run out of steam" and can handle several different tasks at the same time. In fact, they are fun to be around and others tend to find them exciting and interesting.

13. How does having an attention deficit disorder affect a person in school?

ADD can cause significant problems in school. For instance, since children with ADD have trouble paying attention and keeping their mind on their work, they often have to be reminded to listen and to stay on task. More often than not, they have trouble completing their work. Some ADD children who are hyperactive also have trouble sitting still for an entire class period and they find themselves getting restless and fidgety. Further problems result from their impulsivity (excitability and impatience) and resultant tendency to rush through assignments without due care for the neatness or accuracy of their answers. Those with ADD have to try harder in school than others do. They have to remind themselves to pay attention and to be careful when doing their work.

14. How can a student with ADD pay better attention in class?

The first step is to try harder to concentrate. Concentration is an active not a passive process. Maintaining alertness in class can be achieved by following some of these suggestions:

- participate in class discussions
- ask questions when not understanding something
- take notes
- look at the teacher
- do homework the night before so you'll feel involved
- listen to what's going on
- sit near the teacher
- break the daydreaming habit
- try to model other students who are paying attention

15.   How can I develop better study skills?

Developing good study skills is a key to success in school. Try to get into the routine of following these suggestions.

1. Find the best time for you to study. Do it when you are best able to concentrate and when your mind is most receptive to learning information. Some people retain information better when they study at night while others do better in the afternoon or early mornings. Find a comfortable place for studying and use it regularly. The same desk creates familiarity and helps in getting started each time.

2. Set realistic goals. For example, don't force yourself to read an entire chapter in your biology book if your concentration can't last that long. Read what you can, take a break, and read some more later. If you have work to do in several subjects, estimate how long you will need to spend on each assignment.

3. Preview selections or whole chapters in textbooks before reading for details. Move quickly through a chapter skimming much faster than your usual reading rate. The goal is to get an overview of what is important and how the information is presented. Notice all bold-face headings and subheadings. Scan maps, diagrams and illustrations. This should only take a few seconds per page.

4. Read the chapter for the purpose of understanding the material, not to memorize details. Write down

information that you want to remember later. It is important to continually write down such summaries of what you are reading. Get into the habit of reading and writing so you are actively doing something with the information you read.

5. Once you've read the chapter and have taken notes, take a short break. Then go through the chapter and skim it again slowly to refresh your memory. Answer chapter questions. Make sure you have a good understanding of the material. Fill in your notes with additional information you determine to be important.

6. Now put this information into memory. Every once in a while use visualization to remember details. While seated, close your eyes and picture a blank screen in your mind. Picture details of what you want to remember on the mental screen. Focus on the main points. Let the visual image "sink" into your mind. Repeat important statements to yourself and then repeat them out loud. Practice recalling information with and without referring to your notes.

7. Don't just study when you have a test. Reviewing material nightly will make it easier to remember information later in preparation for testing.

16. How can I keep my mind on my homework?

Finding a quiet place at home to work and break-

ing your assignments down into smaller parts sometimes helps.

1. If there is a page or more of problems to do, try
    dividing the assignment into three or four sec-
    tions.
2. Spend ten or fifteen minutes on each section.
    Keep a clock or timer nearby so as to keep track
    of the time.
3. Stop working when the time is up or if you com-
    plete the section.
4. Take a break before using the same procedure
    with the next section of work.

17. How can I keep friends?

     The best way to keep a friend is to be a friend.
While there is no simple formula for making friends or
keeping them, here are a few suggestions that might be
useful.

- A good friend shows caring. Everybody likes to be cared about and when a person shows someone that he/she cares for them they tend to be liked more. There are a lot of ways to show  people you care about them: talking to someone shows care; asking how they are shows care; taking an interest in what they do shows care; going places with them and doing things together shows care.

- A good friend avoids arguments and tries not to blame others. While it is not necessary to agree with everything everyone says or does, it is important to disagree with others in a way which doesn't hurt somebody's feelings.

- A good friend keeps promises. People who say they are going to do one thing and end up doing another usually do not make great friends. People usually think of them as phonies and do not trust them in the future.

- A good friend recognizes that people sometimes need space and gives it to them. Probably one of the biggest problems that ADD children have in keeping friends is that they overwhelm others. This is easy to do when hyperactive. Hyperactivity can cause someone to be too excitable, too opinionated, too bossy, or too impatient with others. Needless to say, most friends won't be too happy about that and will probably want to have contact in small doses only. If one is coming on too strong, take a step back, calm down and start all over again.

• A good friend takes an interest in what others like. People tend to make friends with others who share common interests. Finding out what a person likes to do is a good way to start conversations and can help when plans are made to get together with one another.

18. How can I be less impulsive?

Psychologists have developed methods to help ADD children "stop and think" before reacting too quickly to a situation. Finding a well thought out solution to a problem, putting that solution into action, and evaluating the success of your behavior requires some advanced planning. Try following these five problem solving steps the next time you face a problem.

Step 1: Ask yourself, what is the problem?

Step 2: Ask yourself, what are some plans I can use to solve the problem?

Step 3: Pick the best plan.

Step 4: Try the plan out.

Step 5: Ask yourself, did the plan work?

It is quite important to think through problems rather than jump to conclusions or make hasty decisions.

19. Can I expect my attention span to improve as I get older?

Yes, you probably can. Experts have studied teenagers with ADD and have followed them as they became adults. They have found that for many people, problems with attention span, hyperactivity, and impulsiveness (impatience) lessen with time.

By all means, remember that having attention deficit disorder is not the "end of the world." You can still succeed in school, go to college if you like, and be successful in your career, even with ADD. It might cause you some trouble here and there, but there's a lot you can do to help yourself succeed and to Make the Grade.

20. Where can a person find more information on ADD?

CH.A.D.D., Children With Attention Deficit Disorders is a national ADD support group. CH.A.D.D. maintains several hundred chapters across the country which provide support and information to families and professionals.

Write or call for information:

CH.A.D.D.

499 Northwest 70th Avenue

Plantation, Florida 33317

(305) 587-3700

Making The Grade is a heartwarming story of seventh grader Jim Jerome's struggle to succeed in school. With the help of his parents, teachers and concerned health care professionals Jim learns about ADD and ways to help himself.

Commonly Asked Questions About ADD offers direct information to young readers. Symptoms, causes, treatments, and outcomes of ADD are discussed frankly and positively. Helpful ideas for developing good study and homework habits, improving social skills, and reducing impulsive thinking are presented.

This story is all about me. I knew I had problems paying attention in school. Now I know what I can do to help myself.
.... Jeff, age 13

My brother and I read this story together. It helped me understand him better.
.... Janet, age 15

About the authors.....

Roberta Parker taught middle and junior high school students in New York, Maryland and Florida. She has drawn upon a decade of experiences in teaching children with attention deficit disorder to write this fictional but realistic story.

Harvey C. Parker, Ph.D. is a clinical psychologist in practice in Plantation, Florida. A former teacher and co-founder of CH.A.D.D., a support group for persons living with attention deficit disorders, Dr. Parker lectures nationally on the subject of ADD and educational and behavioral problems of childhood and adolescence.

For a complete catalog of books, audio, and video tapes on attention deficit disorder.
A.D.D. WareHouse • (800) ADD-WARE • (305) 792-8944